SUSAN HILL

I m the King of the Castle

Retold by Jim Alderson

MACMILLAN
MODERN

INTERMEDIATE LEVEL

Series Editor: John Milne

The Macmillan Guided Readers provide a choice of enjoyable reading material for learners of English. The series is published at five levels: Starter, Beginner, Elementary, Intermediate and Upper. At **Intermediate Level**, the control of content and language has the following main features:

Information Control

Information which is vital to the understanding of the story is presented in an easily assimilated manner and is repeated when necessary. Difficult allusion and metaphor are avoided and cultural backgrounds are made explicit.

Structure Control

Most of the structures used in the Readers will be familiar to students who have completed an elementary course of English. Other grammatical features may occur, but their use is made clear through context and reinforcement. This ensures that the reading, as well as being enjoyable, provides a continual learning situation for the students. Sentences are limited in most cases to a maximum of three clauses and within sentences there is a balanced use of adverbial and adjectival phrases. Great care is taken with pronoun reference.

Vocabulary Control

There is a basic vocabulary of approximately 1,600 words. Help is given to the students in the form of illustrations, which are closely related to the text.

Glossary

Some difficult words and phrases in this book are important for understanding the story. Some of these words are explained in the story, some are shown in the pictures, and others are marked with a number like this ...[3] Words with a number are explained in the Glossary on page 75.

Contents

A Note About This Story

The title of the story, *I'm the King of the Castle*, comes from the words used in an English children's game. The children race to climb up a rock or a wall. The boy or girl who gets to the top first shouts out: 'I'm the King of the Castle!' This person is the winner. The two boys in the story struggle with each other to see who is the stronger – who can beat the other. They are fighting each other to see who is the king of the castle.

The story takes place during the long summer holidays. The boys have long holidays because they are both at boarding school. At a day school, the students go home every evening. But at boarding schools the students go home only during the holidays. At boys' boarding schools, the students' first names are never used. The students call each other by their family names. This is why Charles Kingshaw always calls Edmund Hooper 'Hooper' and Edmund Hooper always calls Charles Kingshaw 'Kingshaw'.

1

The House

Edmund Hooper was eleven years old. His mother and grand-mother were dead and Edmund lived with his father. One day, Edmund Hooper's father came home very worried.

'Edmund,' he said. 'Your grandfather is dying. We must go and visit him at once.'

When they arrived at the old man's house, Mr Hooper took Edmund to see his grandfather.

'Don't be afraid, Edmund,' Mr Hooper said. 'Your grandfather is very old and he is dying.'

'I'm never afraid,' said Edmund.

They went into the bedroom. But the old man could not speak. He was breathing noisily and the room smelt unpleasant.

Mr Hooper looked unhappy. 'Your grandfather is very ill,' he said, 'but I wanted you to see him.'

'Why?' asked Edmund.

'You are his grandson,' said Mr Hooper. 'When he dies we will live in this house. And one day it will be yours.'

Edmund looked at the old man. His grandfather's skin was old and dry. The old man's face was thin and grey.

Edmund turned away and walked out of the room. The old man died later that day.

Mr Hooper and Edmund went to live in the big house. It was now their home.

On the first day, Edmund walked all round the old house. It was a tall, ugly building made of dark red brick. The house was very large and there were no other houses near it. There were gardens all around the house. At the back of the house, there were some trees and bushes. A narrow path went through the trees into a small wood[1].

Then Edmund looked inside the house. There were lots of rooms and they all had high ceilings[2]. The walls and doors of the rooms were made of dark brown wood. Edmund wanted a room of his own. He chose a room at the back of the house. It was a dark, narrow room with a tall window. Through the window, Edmund could see the small wood.

One night, Edmund got out of bed. The moon was very large and a warm wind was blowing through the trees. Edmund walked quietly along the passage and down the wide wooden stairs. He walked across the hall[3] and took a key from a desk. The key had red paint on it. This was the key to the Red Room. Edmund walked back across the hall and stood in front of a large door. He unlocked the door and went inside.

The room was like a museum[4]. There were shelves of books and glass cases[5]. The cases were full of his grandfather's moths and butterflies[6]. On the shelves were the bodies of stuffed animals[7]. Edmund's grandfather had been a famous collector[8].

Edmund walked up and down the room very quietly. Then he stopped in front of a glass case at the end of the room. He looked down at the moths and butterflies inside. Then he lifted up the top of the case. As he did this, there was an unpleasant smell.

There was a very large moth in the middle of the case. The boy put out his hand and touched the body of the moth with his finger. At once, the moth became dark dust.

Suddenly Edmund thought of his dead grandfather.

―――――

Next day, Mr Hooper spoke to his son.

'Edmund,' he said. 'I want to talk to you.'

The boy looked at his father and waited.

'I will often have to go to London,' said Mr Hooper. 'I do not like leaving you on your own. Someone is coming here to look after us in this house. Her name is Mrs Kingshaw. She has a boy the same age as you, called Charles.'

Edmund said nothing, but his face was angry.

'You will have a friend to play with during the long school holidays,' said Mr Hooper.

'I don't want a friend.'

'Don't argue[9] with me, Edmund,' said his father. 'I am very busy. I have no time to argue.'

Mr Hooper watched Edmund walk away. The boy looked like his mother. Mrs Hooper had died six years ago. Mr Hooper had not loved his wife and the marriage had never been happy.

Edmund went slowly to his room. He became more and more angry. He did not want things to change. He did not want anyone to come to the house.

2

The Kingshaws

Edmund was upstairs in his bedroom when the Kingshaws arrived. He was making a map[10]. The map showed a battle between two armies.

'Edmund!' his father called. 'Your friend has arrived. I want you to come down at once.'

Edmund quickly wrote something on a small piece of paper. He fixed it to some plasticine[11]. Then he went to the window and looked down at the Kingshaws. They were getting out of a car. He saw an eleven-year-old boy with red hair. Very carefully, Edmund dropped the plasticine out of the window. It fell near the other boy's feet. Edmund moved away from the window. Charles Kingshaw bent down to pick up the plasticine.

Mrs Kingshaw and Mr Hooper smiled at each other. Suddenly the woman turned towards her son.

'What have you got in your hand?' asked Mrs Kingshaw.

'Nothing,' said the boy.

The man and woman walked into the house. Charles followed them. He looked at the piece of paper. It said: I DID NOT WANT YOU TO COME HERE.

'I will take you to your rooms,' said Mr Hooper.

Charles put the paper into his pocket. He was afraid.

———

Some time later, Edmund Hooper went to Charles Kingshaw's room.

'Why have you come here?' he said.

Kingshaw was surprised. He did not answer. He stepped back as the other boy came towards him.

8

He went to the window and looked down at the Kingshaws.

'You're scared[12] of me,' said Hooper.

'I'm not!'

'This house will be mine when my father dies,' Hooper said. 'It will all be mine.'

'That's nothing,' Kingshaw said. 'It's an ugly old house.'

Hooper was angry. 'There's something very valuable[13] downstairs,' he said. 'Something you've never seen before.'

'What is it?'

Hooper smiled and looked out of the window. He was thinking about the collection of moths in the Red Room. But he did not tell Kingshaw about it.

'My grandfather died in this room,' said Hooper. 'He died in that bed. Now it's your bed.'

This was a lie[14], but Kingshaw believed it. He felt afraid.

'Where did you live before you came here?' asked Hooper.

'In a house in London.'

'Was it your house?'

'No.'

Hooper looked coldly at Kingshaw. 'Why didn't your father buy a house?'

'My father is dead.' Kingshaw was angry. He wanted to fight Hooper, but he was afraid.

'Do you remember your father?'

'Yes,' said Kingshaw. 'He was a pilot in the war. I've got a photograph of him.'

'I don't believe you,' said Hooper. 'The war was years and years ago.'

Kingshaw showed the photograph to the other boy. Hooper looked at it. He saw a photograph of a thin man with no hair.

'He's old,' said Hooper.

'I know,' said Kingshaw. 'But he was very young during the war.'

Hooper threw the photograph onto the bed and walked over to the window. 'Where do you go to school?' he said.

'In Wales.'

'Is it a boarding school[15]?' said Hooper.

'Yes.'

'Boarding schools are expensive,' said Hooper. 'How can your mother pay to send you to boarding school?'

'She doesn't pay anything,' said Kingshaw. 'I think it's free.'

'Boarding schools are never free,' said Hooper.

'My father paid all the money before he died,' said Kingshaw. It was a lie and he was ashamed[16].

Hooper looked at the other boy. He knew it was a lie. He had won.

'I didn't want to come here,' said Kingshaw. 'I don't like this place.'

Hooper thought for a moment. He did not like the house either. He pushed open the window and looked outside. The sky was a grey colour. It had been raining. The grass was shining and wet.

'Shut that window,' said Kingshaw suddenly. 'It's my window now.'

Hooper turned round quickly. He was very angry. He ran towards Kingshaw and hit him very hard.

The boys did not speak during the fight. It was a hard fight but it did not last long. Kingshaw wiped[17] the blood from his nose. He was breathing quickly.

Hooper stood by the window and watched him. There was a mark on the side of his face where Kingshaw had hit him. Hooper stood for a moment, then walked slowly across the room. When he got to the door he turned.

'You are not wanted here, Kingshaw,' he said. 'It's not your house.'

Kingshaw stood without moving after Hooper had gone. There was no one in the house who would be his friend. He was going to be very lonely during the long summer holiday. Kingshaw began to cry quietly. He hated his mother. Why had she brought him to this place? He hated the way his mother smiled at Mr Hooper. He was ashamed of her. He walked slowly to the window and shut it.

'It is my window now,' he said.

The boy looked at the bed. He remembered what Hooper had told him. Hooper's grandfather had died in the bed. Kingshaw was afraid.

3
The Crow

Kingshaw and his mother had been in the house for a week.
Kingshaw was very unhappy. He hated Hooper and he
was afraid of him. But Mrs Kingshaw wanted to stay. She told
Kingshaw to be polite to Mr Hooper. She made her son play
with Edmund. But when their parents were not looking, Hooper
was unkind to Kingshaw and followed him everywhere. One day,
Kingshaw found a map and went out for a walk. He decided to go
to a place called Hang Wood.

First, Kingshaw came to a field of grass. He was wearing
sandals on his feet and the thick grass hurt his feet. He was not
interested in where he was going. He wanted to get away from the
ugly house and from Hooper.

Next, he came to a field of yellow corn[18]. The stalks of corn
were growing close together. He saw that someone had been
through the field and had made a path. Kingshaw stopped. He
was worried. Perhaps he should not be walking through the field.
But he went on.

The cornfield was on the top of a hill. The sun was very hot.
Kingshaw could feel sweat[19] on his back and legs. His face felt hot
and uncomfortable. He sat down and looked at the dark trees
at the edge of Hang Wood. The trees seemed very close. He
could see each branch clearly. The fields around him were
very quiet.

Then a crow[20] came.

At first, Kingshaw did not worry about the bird. He had seen
several crows in the fields. But this one flew quietly down into the
corn. It had huge black wings. It flew up again quickly and went
round in a circle over the boy's head. Then the bird dived[21]. It
landed near Kingshaw. The boy could see the feathers shining on

13

its head.

The crow flew up and dived again, but this time it did not land. It was the largest crow the boy had ever seen. Its wings made a loud noise above his head. As the boy looked up, he saw the bird's mouth open. The inside of its mouth was red and it had small, shining eyes.

Kingshaw was frightened and began to run back through the corn. He climbed a gate and jumped down into the grass field on the other side. Sweat was going into his eyes. He looked up. The crow was following him. Kingshaw ran.

The crow went round in a circle and began to dive again. As he ran, Kingshaw began to cry. Tears and sweat covered his face.

Then Kingshaw saw the back of the house and he began to run much faster. But suddenly, he fell. He lay on the ground breathing quickly. He could not get up.

With a loud cry and a terrible noise of its wings, the crow dived down. It landed in the middle of Kingshaw's back.

The boy was too afraid to move. He lay in the field with his eyes closed. He felt the feet of the bird go through his shirt onto his skin. He began to scream[22]. He remembered stories about birds attacking people's eyes. He waited for the crow to attack him.

But after a few moments, the bird flew up again. Kingshaw got up and ran. The bird followed him, but it was silent now. It made no noise and it did not dive down.

Kingshaw climbed over a fence[23] and ran to the house. He turned round. The crow was flying away. The boy wiped his face with his hand. He was trembling[24].

Then Kingshaw looked up at the house. Hooper was standing at the window of his bedroom, watching him.

It landed in the middle of Kingshaw's back.

4
'I Dare You!'

Hooper came into Kingshaw's room.
'You were scared,' he said. 'You were running away.'

'This is my room,' said Kingshaw. 'I don't want you here, Hooper.'

'You should lock the door then.'

'There isn't a key.'

Hooper smiled. 'You were scared of a little bird!' he said.

'I was not!'

'You were crying. I know you were crying.'

'Shut up, shut up.'

'Haven't you seen a crow before?' Hooper said. 'Did it frighten you? Did you cry for your mother?'

Kingshaw turned round quickly. He did not like what Hooper was saying.

'Where were you going?' asked Hooper.

'I'm not telling you. I don't have to tell you anything,' said Kingshaw.

Hooper was angry now. He pushed Kingshaw back against the wall.

'Be careful what you say to me!'

Kingshaw bit Hooper's hand. Hooper stepped back. But he went on looking at Kingshaw.

'You were going to Hang Wood, weren't you?'

Kingshaw did not reply.

'You're scared of the wood,' said Hooper. 'I dare[25] you to go into Hang Wood. I dare you!'

'Shut up!'

'You're scared,' said Hooper again. 'I dare you to go into Hang Wood.'

'Oh, go away!'

Hooper looked at Kingshaw for a moment, then suddenly left the room.

Kingshaw knew he would have to go to Hang Wood. He was afraid, but he knew he had to go.

———

Kingshaw woke during the night. There was a noise outside his bedroom door. Kingshaw opened his eyes. The moon was shining into his room and he could see something on his bed. At first he did not know what it was.

Kingshaw switched on the light by the side of his bed. Then he looked.

The big black crow was not alive. He knew at once that it was dead. It was a stuffed crow. But its feet were holding the sheet. And it had shining eyes.

Kingshaw was terrified. He could not move. But he did not scream. He knew Hooper had done this. Hooper was outside waiting for Kingshaw to cry out. Kingshaw switched off the light and lay with his eyes tightly shut. He wanted to die and he wanted Hooper to die too. But there was nothing he could do, nothing. After a long time, he went to sleep.

When he woke up again, it was six o'clock in the morning. He could see the crow clearly but – he was very frightened. He lay and waited for the bird to move. He waited for it to fly up and attack his eyes.

I'm being stupid, Kingshaw thought. It's dead. It's a stuffed, dead bird.

He moved carefully out of bed and onto the floor. Then he ran. He sat for a long time in the bathroom. The house was silent.

When he got back to his bedroom, the crow had gone.

5
The Red Room

During breakfast, Hooper looked at Kingshaw's face. He wanted to know what Kingshaw was thinking. But Kingshaw did not look at Hooper and he did not speak.

After breakfast, Kingshaw went into the garden. He wanted to get away from Hooper. He walked down the path and then stopped. He was standing outside the Red Room. He put his face to the window. He tried to look through the glass.

He did not hear Hooper walk up behind him.

'What are you doing?' Hooper asked.

Kingshaw turned round quickly.

'You can't get in there,' said Hooper. 'That room's locked. It's the Red Room. My father has the key.'

'Why?' Kingshaw looked through the window again. 'I can only see a lot of old books.'

Hooper smiled. 'There are valuable things in there. Things you have never seen.'

Kingshaw was interested, but he moved away from the window.

'Do you want me to show you?' asked Hooper.

Kingshaw said nothing. Hooper was clever. He must never let Hooper know what he was thinking.

'You can come with me after supper,' said Hooper.

———

After supper, Kingshaw stood in the hall and waited. Suddenly Hooper walked up behind him.

'I've got the key,' he said.

It was dark inside the Red Room. Outside, the sky was grey and it was raining. The branches of the trees moved against the windows.

Kingshaw went into the room and stopped. He looked at the glass cases. He did not like this place.

'Go on,' said Hooper. 'Have a look.'

Kingshaw moved slowly towards the glass cases. Then he took a quick breath.

'Moths!' he said.

'Yes, moths from every part of the world.'

'Where did they come from?'

'My grandfather collected them,' said Hooper. 'My grandfather was the most famous collector in the world. He wrote lots of books about moths.'

Kingshaw looked at the dead moths. He was terrified of moths. He was terrified of the way they moved. He hated being touched by their wings.

Hooper came up behind him.

'Go on. Open one of the cases.'

'No!'

'Why not? Are you scared of a moth?'

'No!'

Hooper pushed open one of the cases.

'Pick one up.'

Kingshaw moved away. He did not dare touch a moth. He did not want Hooper to touch one.

'What's the matter?' asked Hooper.

Kingshaw went on moving backwards. He wanted to get out of the room.

'Come here and look, Kingshaw.'

'I don't want to.'

'I'm going to pick one up. I'm not scared.'

'No, don't!'

'Why not?' Hooper said.

'Come here and look, Kingshaw.'

'They're valuable,' said Kingshaw quickly. 'Your father will be angry.'

Suddenly Hooper ran past Kingshaw. He went out of the door and turned the key. Kingshaw was locked in.

Kingshaw ran to the windows. He pushed and pushed at the windows but they would not open. He did not dare to turn round. He could not look at the hundreds of moths lying in their glass cases. He knew they were watching him.

Kingshaw waited and waited but no one came. He did not want to call out. He did not want Hooper to know that he had won.

It was dark now. Kingshaw switched on a small light. At once, a live moth flew against the light. It touched his hand and flew round and round …

———

At last Kingshaw heard Mr Hooper and his mother in the hall. He called out and they opened the door.

'I got locked in,' he said, 'I'm all right now. Goodnight.'

Then he ran up the stairs before they could ask any questions.

That night, Kingshaw lay in bed thinking.

'Oh God,' he said. 'Make Mr Hooper send us away.'

He wanted to get away from Edmund Hooper. He wanted the summer holidays to end. He wanted to go back to St Vincent's School. He was happy there.

6

Kingshaw's Plan

Kingshaw hated Hooper. He had never hated anyone so much before. One day, when Hooper was in London with his father, Kingshaw looked into all the rooms in the house. He found a small room that he liked very much. There was a lock on the door with a key in it.

Kingshaw took his model[26] ship into the room. He liked working alone. He felt safe[27] when he was alone.

Hooper knew that Kingshaw had a secret[28] room. In the next few days, Hooper looked for Kingshaw everywhere.

Kingshaw knew that Hooper would find his secret room. He knew he had to get away from Hooper, so Kingshaw began to make a plan. He was going to run away[29]. In a few days he was almost ready to go.

Kingshaw had two more things to take to the secret room. He waited until after lunch, then he walked up the stairs. He wanted to put the things in his small bag.

But Hooper was waiting outside the secret room. He was sitting on the floor with his back against the door. Kingshaw stopped.

'Are you going somewhere?' Hooper asked.

'Go away, Hooper,' said Kingshaw.

'This isn't your house,' said Hooper. 'And this isn't your room. I want to know what you have in here.'

Kingshaw said nothing. Hooper would get into the room. Hooper always won.

Kingshaw slowly put his hand into the pocket of his jeans. He took out the key and opened the door.

Hooper stepped inside the room.

'What do you come in here for?' he asked.

There was silence.

'What's in that bag?' Hooper asked. Before Kingshaw could stop him, Hooper began to open the small green bag on the floor.

Kingshaw turned away and put his hands in his pockets. Hooper placed all the things on a table.

'You stole[30] these,' Hooper said. 'You're a thief!'

Kingshaw turned round. Hooper was looking down at the matches. He understood now. 'You're planning to go to ...' He stopped speaking and looked at Kingshaw. 'I know why you're doing it,' Hooper said. 'You're scared of me, Kingshaw.'

'Don't be stupid.'

But Hooper was laughing. He knew he was right. He went to the door and then looked at Kingshaw.

'I shall come with you,' he said.

Then Hooper left the room.

Kingshaw knew he had to escape from Hooper. Kingshaw hated him. If Kingshaw did not get away, things would get worse.

Hooper was clever but he did not know everything. He did not know all of Kingshaw's plan.

Mr Hooper liked Mrs Kingshaw very much. He enjoyed talking to her in the evenings.

'You have made me feel very happy,' he said. 'I don't feel so lonely now.'

Mr Hooper and Mrs Kingshaw spent more and more time together. They wanted the boys to be friends too. But they did not know the truth.

Mrs Kingshaw was very pleased. Mr Hooper likes me, she thought. My life is changing. I was right to come here.

One evening, Mrs Kingshaw spoke to her son.

'I'm going to London tomorrow,' she said. She smiled at Mr Hooper. She was very excited. 'We will bring you back a present,' she said.

Kingshaw said nothing. He was ashamed of his mother. He hated the way she smiled at Mr Hooper. But this was his chance. He was going to run away.

7

Hang Wood

Kingshaw had put everything he needed into his bag. He had some biscuits, some cheese, chocolate and sweets. He had a torch, a pair of socks and a ball of string. And he had some money, more than seven pounds. He was not going to take any water. He would drink a lot before he went.

He was going to Crelford Station to catch a train. He was not going to the station by road. He thought someone might see him. He decided to walk across the fields. On the way to Crelford, he would go to Hang Wood. That was something he had to do. He had been dared to do it by Hooper.

As Kingshaw went upstairs, he saw Hooper standing outside his bedroom door. Hooper looked at Kingshaw carefully. Kingshaw was worried. Perhaps Hooper knew what he was going to do.

But I shall be gone tomorrow, thought Kingshaw. I will be far away from Hooper.

Kingshaw got into bed. He was going to get up at five o'clock. He was going to leave the house before his mother and Mr Hooper went to London.

Kingshaw had never been up so early before. He felt very strange. When he reached the first field, he turned to look back at the house. All its windows were shut. It was a very ugly place. Kingshaw hated it.

It was cold and the long grass was wet. Soon Kingshaw's jeans were wet too.

He came to the place where he had fallen and the crow had

dived onto his back. He remembered the bird's feet on his skin and he shivered[31]. But he walked on through the field. There was no sound.

Kingshaw looked back towards the house again and again. But no one was following him. He thought of his mother in her new green dress. He thought of Mr Hooper. He was thin and dark like a crow.

By the time Kingshaw had reached Hang Wood, the sun was high in the sky. But it was very cold. Kingshaw knew he had to go into the wood. Hooper had dared him to do it.

It was not easy to get into Hang Wood. There was a ditch[32], a line of bushes and a wire fence. Kingshaw stopped for a moment, then he saw a way in through the bushes.

He took a few steps forward with his eyes closed. When he opened his eyes, he was in Hang Wood!

Kingshaw looked around him. The sun was shining through the trees. Kingshaw was happy. No one would find him in the wood. He was safe. He touched the trees and he touched the grass. Birds were singing and moving in the trees.

Kingshaw ate some food. He wanted to drink, so he went to find some water. He walked on and on into the wood. The trees were growing close together and the wood was darker. It was very hot and Kingshaw was sweating. He stopped to wipe his face.

Then he heard a sound. He listened and heard the sound again. It came from behind him. Kingshaw went behind a bush and waited.

The wood was quiet. Then the bushes moved and there was Hooper!

Kingshaw did not make a sound. There was a long silence, then Hooper spoke.

'You can come out, Kingshaw,' he said. 'I can see your feet behind that bush.'

Kingshaw stood up very slowly and the two boys looked at each other.

Then the bushes moved and there was Hooper!

'You can't get away from me,' said Hooper. 'I'm going with you.'

'You don't know where I'm going,' Kingshaw said. 'You can't come with me, Hooper. You ...'

'Yes, I can,' said Hooper. 'I can do anything.'

'Shut up, Hooper,' said Kingshaw.

Hooper smiled. 'Your mother is a servant. You must do what I tell you. You can't stop me from coming with you.'

Kingshaw wanted to hit Hooper. He wanted to hit him and hit him. At last he turned round and began to walk quickly through the wood. Hooper followed him. Kingshaw was unhappy, but he was not frightened of Hooper now. Kingshaw liked being in the wood.

The trees were very close together now. It was much hotter and the boys could not breathe easily. Kingshaw was sweating and his shirt was wet. Suddenly the boys heard a sound.

'What is it?' asked Kingshaw.

'I don't know. It must be an animal,' replied Hooper.

They were both afraid. After a time, Kingshaw walked forward. They heard the sound again. Kingshaw pushed through some bushes.

A large animal was standing in a clearing[33]. The animal was brown with large, shining eyes. It was very frightened.

'It's a deer,' Kingshaw said.

'Let's follow it,' said Hooper. 'We might see hundreds and hundreds of them.'

Kingshaw followed Hooper. They went on and on into the wood. Hooper walked in front and he decided where they were going.

Kingshaw was hot and tired. He looked at his watch. It was eight o'clock. They had been in the wood for two hours.

'I don't want to play this game now,' he said.

Kingshaw walked away and Hooper walked slowly after him. After a long time, Kingshaw stopped and looked around.

'We're lost,' said Kingshaw. 'I don't know where we are. We'll stay here and think of a plan.'

Hooper sat down on the ground. He was crying.

'You brought me here, Kingshaw,' he said. 'Why did you make me come?'

'Shut up!'

From somewhere far away, came the sound of thunder[34].

8

The Storm

'That was thunder,' said Hooper.
      'Yes. There's a storm coming.'
   Hooper's face was very white.
   'Thunderstorms make me ill,' he said. 'I hate them.'
   Kingshaw was surprised. Hooper's scared, he thought. He's very scared.
   They heard the thunder again, not far away.
   'I hate thunder. It makes me sick,' Hooper said.
   Kingshaw did not feel sorry for the other boy, but he said nothing.
   The sky became dark and the air was very hot. Kingshaw knew that the storm would come soon, but he was not afraid.
   Suddenly, the thunder was above their heads. Hooper jumped up and looked all around. He was terrified.
   'Come on,' said Kingshaw. 'It's going to rain. Get under these bushes.'
   At first, Hooper did not move, then he began to shiver. There was a flash of lightning and the trees shone white.
   The two boys got under the bushes. Hooper lay on the ground; he could not stop shivering. When the thunder came again, he put his fingers in his ears.
   'It's nothing,' said Kingshaw. 'It's only thunder.'
   There was another flash of lightning.
   'Oh God, oh God!' Hooper was terrified.
   Kingshaw remembered that he had been afraid of the crow. He was sorry for Hooper.
   'The storm will go away soon,' Kingshaw said.
   But Hooper did not hear him; he was too afraid.
   The rain came slowly at first. Then it fell faster and faster. The

trees and bushes were wet and there was water on the ground. The rain and thunder made a terrible sound. Hooper cried out and moved from side to side.

Hooper won't be able to frighten me again, Kingshaw thought. He won't frighten me any more.

It was a long time before the thunder moved away. Then, suddenly, the sun was shining. It shone on the wet ground and the wet trees. Kingshaw stood up. 'Come on, Hooper,' he said. 'It's safe now.'

The birds were singing again. Water dropped from the trees and onto the ground. But Hooper did not move. He sat for a long time listening for any sound of the storm.

Then Kingshaw heard the sound of moving water.

'I can hear a stream[35],' he said to Hooper. 'I want a drink. I'm going to find the stream.'

Hooper stood up and looked all around. He picked up Kingshaw's bag.

'Yes,' he said. 'I can hear the stream. It's over there. I'll go first. Follow me.'

Kingshaw did not argue. He was too surprised.

They found the stream and followed it for about three kilometres. The ground was wet and muddy[36]. There was an unpleasant smell. They did not see any birds or butterflies. The trees were dark and frightening.

Suddenly, Hooper stopped.

'Let's go back,' he said. 'I hate this place. It's getting darker and darker.'

But Kingshaw went on walking. 'You're stupid,' he said. 'We must follow the stream.'

They walked on through the trees and bushes. At last they came to a clearing.

There was a pool at one end of the clearing. Further on, they could see more trees.

For a moment they stood there. They did not know what to do.

Then the sun began to shine and the clearing was full of light. The water of the stream and the pond was bright and clean.

Hooper threw the bag on the ground. 'I'm going for a swim,' he said.

9

The Pool

Hooper took off his clothes and threw them onto the grass. He ran to the bank[37] of the stream and jumped in. He began to jump about in the water.

'Come on, Kingshaw, it's great!'

Hooper hit the water with his hands.

'What's wrong?' he shouted. 'Can't you swim? It's not cold.'

Kingshaw took off his clothes carefully and put them on top of his bag. He walked across the cold ground towards the pool. Hooper began to make a lot of noise.

Kingshaw suddenly felt very happy. With a loud shout he jumped into the stream.

The water was warm. Kingshaw put his head under the water and began to swim. The water was green and there were fish in it.

The boys were in the water for a long time. They washed the mud off their legs and ran through the stream shouting and laughing.

This is great, thought Kingshaw.

The sun was not shining now. They came out of the water and onto the bank. They began to shiver. They were cold and wet.

'We must make a fire,' said Kingshaw. 'I've got some matches. We must get some large stones from the pool. If we put them here, we can make the fire inside them.'

Kingshaw started to put the stones into a circle. He was happy now. He was not afraid of Hooper.

Hooper was behind Kingshaw. He was lifting up a big stone from the pool.

'Be quick!' said Kingshaw.

At once, Kingshaw knew that he had made a mistake[38]. He

The boys were in the water for a long time.

looked back. Hooper was watching him. He walked towards Kingshaw with slow steps.

'Don't tell me what to do, Kingshaw.'

'We've got to make this fire,' Kingshaw replied.

'I can make you afraid of me,' said Hooper. 'You know that, don't you?'

'Oh shut up, Hooper. I'm not afraid of you.'

'Yes, you are,' said Hooper. 'You've always been scared of me. That's why you ran away.'

Kingshaw got up and went to the stream for another stone. Hooper followed him.

'We might have to stay here for hours,' said Hooper. 'We will have to keep the fire burning.'

'Of course,' said Kingshaw.

'Then the moths will come,' said Hooper quietly. 'Big ones. There are always moths in woods.'

Kingshaw felt ill. He remembered the smell of the Red Room.

Hooper smiled and walked away.

'I'm not frightened of stupid moths,' Kingshaw shouted. 'You don't scare me.'

Hooper turned round and smiled again.

Kingshaw did not speak. He was very angry. Hooper had won.

10

Kingshaw Goes Off Alone

'What time is it?' asked Hooper. Kingshaw looked at his watch. 'Three o'clock,' he said.

Hooper sat down beside the stones. 'What are we going to do?' he asked.

'Make a fire.'

'Then what will we do?' Hooper asked.

'We'll eat. I'll catch a fish and cook it.'

'How are we going to get out of here?'

'We'll go on walking,' replied Kingshaw. 'It's not a big wood.'

Hooper began to tremble. 'But this isn't Hang Wood,' he said. 'It's Barnard's Forest!'

'What?'

'We've got into Barnard's Forest by mistake. The Forest goes on for miles and miles.'

Hooper's face was white. 'They'll never find us!' he cried. 'They'll never find us.'

Kingshaw did not answer. Suddenly Hooper fell to the ground. He hit the ground with his hands. Then he began to scream.

'Stop it,' Kingshaw said. 'Stop it, Hooper. Don't be stupid.'

But Hooper could not stop. He screamed louder and louder. Kingshaw pushed him on to his back and hit him across his face again and again.

'Stop it, Hooper!' he shouted. 'Stop doing that!'

Hooper stopped. Kingshaw moved away slowly. He had touched Hooper. He did not like it.

Hooper did not move for a long time. Then he turned over and pushed his face into the ground. He began to cry.

Then Kingshaw remembered something. He went to his bag and took out the ball of string.

'I've got an idea,' said Kingshaw. 'I'm going to tie some string to a tree. Then I'll go and see if we're near the end of the wood.'

'Don't go,' said Hooper. 'Something might happen.'

'What?'

'I don't know. Anything might happen.'

Kingshaw began to walk away.

'I'll leave the matches. You can light the fire,' said Kingshaw. Hooper said nothing.

Kingshaw went to the end of the clearing. He tied the string to a tree. Then he walked through the trees, holding the ball of string in his hands.

Kingshaw was happy. He was not afraid of the wood and he liked being alone. When he came to the end of the string, he stopped and thought about Hooper. Hooper hated being left alone. Hooper would be terrified if he did not go back. Kingshaw was afraid of Hooper, but he knew he would have to return. He turned round. He followed the string through the trees. As he walked he made the string into a ball again.

When he got back to the clearing, he could not see Hooper.

'Hooper!' shouted Kingshaw.

Then he saw a foot on the bank of the stream. Hooper must be fishing, thought Kingshaw.

'You're stupid, Hooper,' shouted Kingshaw, 'You're …'

He stopped suddenly.

'Oh God!'

Hooper was lying in the stream. There was some blood on the water. It had come from Hooper's head.

'Oh God, oh God …'

Kingshaw jumped into the water and put his hands under Hooper's head. Hooper had hit his head on a stone. There was a big cut on Hooper's face. Blood was running out of the cut. But the stone had kept his face above the water.

Kingshaw pulled Hooper onto the bank. Then he put Hooper on his side and began to push down on his back. Kingshaw pushed again and again. Nothing happened. Then water came from Hooper's mouth and nose. His eyes opened, then they shut again and he lay still.

Kingshaw lit the fire. If Hooper died, it would be his fault. Kingshaw shivered.

Suddenly Hooper made a noise. Kingshaw turned round and saw him sitting up.

'Are you all right?' said Kingshaw, sitting down beside him. 'Oh, God, I thought you were dead, Hooper.'

'I tried to catch a fish, but I fell … My head hurts. I want a drink.'

Kingshaw brought Hooper some water in a small cup. He put some aspirin[39] in the water. Hooper drank it. Kingshaw was happy, now because Hooper was alive.

Hooper suddenly became angry and frightened. 'Have you found a way out of the wood?' he asked. 'If you get out and leave me here, I'll kill you.'

'I don't know where we are,' Kingshaw said. 'We're lost.'

It began to get dark. Kingshaw caught a fish and tried to cook it. But the fish tasted bad.

'That was horrible,' said Hooper. 'You're stupid, Kingshaw. You can't do anything.

'You shouldn't have left me,' he went on. 'I might have died. Then you would be a murderer.'

'Oh shut up, Hooper. You're not dead, so stop being stupid.'

As it grew darker, the fire began to shine very brightly.

'They'll be coming home now,' said Hooper. 'They'll be on the train.'

'Yes.'

'When they get home, your mother will go to your room to kiss you,' said Hooper. 'She has to kiss you goodnight. Kiss, kiss, kiss!'

'You're saying that because you haven't got a mother.'

'I don't want a mother,' Hooper said. 'Fathers are better.'

Hooper looked at the fire before speaking again. 'How many men has your mother tried to marry?' he asked quietly.

'What d'you mean?' Kingshaw wanted to kill Hooper. He wanted to hit him and hit him.

Hooper laughed. 'Your mother wants to marry my father,' he said. 'He's rich, and she wants a house and lots of money.'

'That's a lie!' shouted Kingshaw.

'I know about these things,' said Hooper.

Kingshaw knew it was true. Hooper was right about his mother. Kingshaw was ashamed of her. The boys at school said the same things about her. He wished she was dead.

40

Kingshaw walked slowly away from the fire towards the end of the clearing.

'Where are you going?' shouted Hooper. He was frightened. 'You can't leave me. My head hurts. I feel ill.'

Kingshaw went on walking.

'Don't leave me here,' Hooper cried. 'If you do, I'll find you. Then I'll kill you.'

'You don't frighten me,' Kingshaw said.

'Yes, I do. That's why you ran away. You were frightened of a dead crow.'

'Shut up, Hooper!'

Then Hooper began to cry. 'Don't leave me,' he said. 'Don't, don't, don't!'

Kingshaw was suddenly angry. He ran back and stood by Hooper. 'Shut up, Hooper, shut up!' he shouted. 'Shut up or I'll hit you, I'll hit you on the head!'

Hooper tried to move away.

'Are you going to shut up?' Kingshaw shouted.

'Yes, I. . .'

Kingshaw walked off again, trembling. After a few minutes he went back to Hooper.

'I won't hit you,' he said.

Hooper said nothing, but he lay there, listening to the sounds in the wood.

Kingshaw closed his eyes. What will happen if no one comes? he thought.

11

The Rescue

The boys woke up many times in the night. They heard the sounds of animals and birds in the wood.

Hooper was hot and ill. He asked for water. Kingshaw gave him a drink and some more aspirin.

The boys woke up very early. They watched the sunlight come into the clearing.

'I'll get some wood for the fire,' said Kingshaw, standing up.

Hooper stood up carefully. 'I think I feel better now,' he said.

Kingshaw picked up pieces of wood for the fire and listened to the birds. Then the boys had biscuits and water for breakfast.

'I'm going for a swim,' Kingshaw said. He took off his clothes and lay down in the stream. The sunlight came through the trees. Kingshaw closed his eyes. This is good, he thought. This is good.

All around, the birds were singing.

Then he heard the first shout. He heard the sound of a dog. There was another shout and the dog barked again.

Kingshaw opened his eyes and saw Hooper looking at him.

'Someone's coming,' Hooper said.

Kingshaw said nothing. He closed his eyes again and did not move.

I don't want anyone to come, he thought. I don't want them to find us. I want to stay here.

But he knew they would take him back. For a moment, he was afraid. Then he remembered what Hooper had said and done. Perhaps everything would be all right now.

There was another shout and he opened his eyes. A man was standing on the bank of the stream. He was looking down at Kingshaw.

When they were back in the house, Hooper turned to his father.

'Kingshaw did it. He pushed me in the water.'

Kingshaw was very surprised by Hooper's words.

'That's a lie, Hooper!' he cried. 'I didn't touch you. You fell in.'

Mrs Kingshaw was very unhappy. 'Be quiet, Charles,' she said to her son. 'You mustn't say that. I'm very ashamed of you.'

'He sat on me and hit me,' Hooper shouted.

Kingshaw's mother looked carefully at the cut on Hooper's face. Kingshaw hated her. He hated them all.

'He was trying to catch a fish,' said Kingshaw. 'He fell …'

But Kingshaw knew they would not listen to him. He walked towards the door.

'Charles, come here!' Mrs Kingshaw said. 'I don't want you to go out.'

'Why don't you play with Edmund?' Mr Hooper said quietly.

'Oh, don't be stupid!' Kingshaw said.

'Charles!' cried Mrs Kingshaw.

'I'm not playing with him. I hate him,' Kingshaw replied.

'Charles! Tell Mr Hooper and Edmund you are sorry. Tell them at once. Edmund is your friend.'

Kingshaw wanted to scream. 'I wish he had broken his head open on that stone,' he said. 'I wish he was dead!'

Mrs Kingshaw sat down on a chair. She began to cry.

'I told you!' said Hooper. 'He hit me and pushed me in the water.'

'Lies, lies, lies!' Kingshaw ran towards Hooper. But Mr Hooper held Kingshaw's arm with his long, thin fingers.

'I am ashamed of you both,' said Mr Hooper. 'Go to your rooms.'

Mrs Kingshaw wiped her eyes. 'I'm sorry about Charles,' she said. 'I don't understand him.'

'It's all right,' said Mr Hooper quietly. 'Don't worry.'

'You're very kind to us,' Mrs Kingshaw replied.

Kingshaw was ashamed of his mother. He hated the way she was talking to Mr Hooper.

'I want an aspirin,' said Hooper. 'I feel ill.'

Mrs Kingshaw stood up. 'I'll get you one, Edmund,' she said.

'He's not ill,' said Kingshaw. 'He's stupid. He was scared of the storm. He cried.'

'Go to your room!' said Mrs Kingshaw.

Kingshaw turned away. As he walked to the door, Hooper hit Kingshaw's leg. But Kingshaw said nothing.

———

Some time later, Mrs Kingshaw went to her son's room. 'I have come to talk to you, Charles,' she said.

Kingshaw said nothing.

'Mr Hooper has been kind to us. You must not be difficult, Charles. I want us all to be happy. I am so happy now.'

Kingshaw looked at his mother.

'I want you to be Edmund's friend,' she said.

'I hate Hooper. I've told you that before.'

'That's a bad thing to say. Why do you hate him? Tell me, Charles.'

Kingshaw did not want to tell her.

'Mr Hooper and I have a surprise for you,' Mrs Kingshaw said. 'We will tell you what it is tomorrow.'

She kissed her son and then left the room.

They are going to get married, thought Kingshaw. That's the surprise. Hooper will be my brother. Oh God! What am I going to do?

Then Kingshaw remembered the wood. He liked the wood. It was terrifying but it was safe.

12
The Shed

At breakfast the next day, Kingshaw was very unhappy. Was Mr Hooper going to be his father?

When Mr Hooper had finished eating, he smiled. 'Charles,' he said. 'I have something to tell you. Next month, you will not go back to St Vincent's School. You will be going to school with Edmund.'

After breakfast, Kingshaw ran outside. The sun was shining and it was very hot. He had to get away from them all. He hated them.

He ran into the garden. After a few minutes he came to a fence. On the other side of the fence was an old shed[40]. He climbed over the fence and ran towards the shed.

The door of the shed was shut but it opened easily. Kingshaw went in. He was very happy. Hooper would not find him here! It was cold and dark inside the shed. There was a smell of animals. Kingshaw shivered and sat down.

Then suddenly the door shut. Kingshaw jumped up and ran towards the door. But he was too late. When he pushed the door, it did not move.

Kingshaw stood there quietly. Then he said, 'Hooper?'

There was no reply.

'I know it's you!' said Kingshaw.

There was no sound.

'I can get out of here easily,' Kingshaw said.

But he was afraid. Who was outside? Who had shut the door?

Kingshaw turned away from the door. He sat down again. Then something ran over his hand. He screamed and hit his hand against his jeans again and again. Kingshaw was terrified.

He got up and moved to another part of the shed. He lay down. After a while, he fell asleep.

Kingshaw had a terrifying dream. The dream was about blood and hundreds of black crows flying towards him. Then he heard someone calling his name.

'Kingshaw. Kingshaw.'

Suddenly he woke up.

'Kingshaw …'

It was Hooper. He was laughing.

'I've shut you in,' said Hooper.

'I don't care,' said Kingshaw.

'You're coming to my school,' said Hooper. 'I have many friends there. My friends will do what I tell them. They will do all kinds of things to you.'

'I can tell them about the thunderstorm,' said Kingshaw.

'They won't listen to you,' Hooper replied. 'They'll listen to me, not to you.'

Kingshaw said nothing. He was afraid. He did not want to go to school with Hooper.

'Are you scared in there, Kingshaw?' Hooper said quietly. 'There might be animals in there. There might be a lot of moths.'

Kingshaw did not want to cry. He began to say quietly to himself, 'I'll kill you, Hooper, I'll kill you. I'll kill you.' Then he screamed the words.

There was no sound outside. Kingshaw was crying now. He waited for Hooper to laugh again. But Hooper had gone.

Later he heard someone coming towards the shed. There was a noise and the shed door came open.

Hooper shouted, 'It's time for lunch, stupid. We've got to go somewhere with my father. Be quick.'

Kingshaw got up. He heard Hooper running away through the grass. He wiped his face and walked slowly out of the shed. It was raining.

13

Leydell Castle

After lunch, they all got in the car. It had stopped raining and they were going to Leydell Castle. Mrs Kingshaw was very happy. They were all going to spend the day together.

It was a long journey. Kingshaw and Hooper sat in the back of the car. They did not speak to each other.

At last they saw the ruins[41] of the castle. There were hills and trees all round it. Near the castle there was a large lake[42].

Mr Hooper stopped the car.

'I've brought books and maps about the castle,' said Mr Hooper to Mrs Kingshaw. 'We can read them. And then we can look at the castle together.'

Mrs Kingshaw smiled. She wanted to please Mr Hooper.

Mr Hooper took Mrs Kingshaw to look at the lake. But the boys ran towards the castle.

'What are you going to do?' asked Hooper.

'Climb,' Kingshaw replied.

They were inside the ruins now. The walls were very high and there were many broken stone steps. The stones in the walls were large and grass grew between them.

'I dare you to climb to the top.'

Kingshaw smiled and he began to climb.

'You'll fall off,' said Hooper.

But Kingshaw was not afraid. He looked down at Hooper. 'Why don't you come up too?' he said.

Hooper took a knife out of his pocket and began to cut his name on a stone.

Kingshaw went on climbing. Soon he was very high. He looked down and saw the lake. His mother and Mr Hooper had walked to the other side of the lake. They were sitting on a seat. Kingshaw felt very tall and strong. He felt safe, too. This is great, he thought to himself. He shouted down to Hooper. Hooper looked up.

'I'm the King of the Castle[43]!' shouted Kingshaw. He began to dance on top of the high wall.

Hooper was angry. 'Come down,' he said. 'You think you're great, don't you? If you fall, you'll break your head open.'

'Don't be stupid. I'm not going to fall.'

Kingshaw began to climb higher. He smiled down at Hooper. He knew the other boy was afraid.

'I can come up if I want to,' said Hooper.

'Come on, then,' replied Kingshaw.

'I'm going down to the rooms under the castle. It's dark there. I dare you to come with me.'

Kingshaw laughed. Then suddenly, he jumped from one wall to another. He saw Hooper looking up at him. Hooper's face was white. Kingshaw laughed again and Hooper turned away.

Kingshaw looked at the sky and the trees all around. He saw his mother and Mr Hooper sitting on the seat looking at each other. For a short time, he felt he was higher than anyone in the world. Then he decided to come down.

Suddenly he saw Hooper. He had climbed up to a narrow part of the wall.

'What are you doing?' Kingshaw asked.

'You didn't think I could do it, did you?' said Hooper.

Kingshaw climbed down until he was a little way above Hooper. 'I'm going back now,' he said. 'The food will be ready. Get out of the way.'

Hooper did not answer.

'Come on!'

Hooper did not move. His face had gone white.

'Are you ill or something?'

There was no reply.

'You'll have to get down first, Hooper. I can't get past you.

Hooper looked up. 'I'm the King of the Castle!'
shouted Kingshaw.

The wall is too narrow.'

'I can't!' cried Hooper.

'Why not?'

'I'll fall off!'

Kingshaw was angry. 'Why did you come up here?'

Hooper looked terrified. 'You dared me to climb,' he said.

'No, I didn't!'

'I'll fall off, Kingshaw. I can't hold on.' Hooper's face was white with fear.

Kingshaw thought for a moment. Then he said, 'Listen. I'll try to help you. You must do everything I tell you. Do you understand?'

'Yes.'

'First, take your hands off the wall.'

'I can't!'

'Do as I say,' said Kingshaw.

'If I fall off here, I'll die.'

'TAKE YOUR HANDS OFF THE WALL, HOOPER.'

Slowly, Hooper began to take his fingers off the wall.

'Now open your eyes,' said Kingshaw.

'No.'

'Open your eyes. You've got to see where to put your feet. But don't look down at the ground.'

Hooper opened his eyes. He looked at the ground below. 'Oh God!' he said and closed his eyes again.

Kingshaw looked down at Hooper. I am the King, thought Kingshaw. I can make Hooper fall.

Hooper looked up at Kingshaw. He knew. 'Don't make me fall,' he said. 'Don't make me fall.'

Kingshaw did not speak. He saw his mother and Mr Hooper far below. They were looking at each other. He thought of the dark shed with the smell of animals. 'I'm the King of the Castle now,' he said to himself. 'I can do anything.'

Kingshaw decided to help Hooper. But he had to be careful. He did not want to frighten Hooper.

Kingshaw held out his hand. A look of fear came into Hooper's eyes. He took a step backwards, screamed and fell.

14

Kingshaw's Dreams

Hooper held out one arm as he fell. It was a long, long time before he hit the ground.

Then everything happened quickly. Mr Hooper and Mrs Kingshaw began to run towards Hooper. Other people ran up too. Soon an ambulance arrived. Hooper was lifted into the ambulance. His father got in and the ambulance was driven away.

Hooper's dead, thought Kingshaw. Hooper's dead.

———

Kingshaw's mother took Kingshaw back to the house in Mr Hooper's car. Mrs Kingshaw did not speak to him.

'I didn't push him,' said Kingshaw. 'I didn't touch him. Hooper fell. He was stupid.'

The car arrived at the house. Kingshaw knew that Hooper was dead. He began to be very afraid. What would they do with Hooper now? Would they make Kingshaw look at Hooper's dead body?

His mother gave him a drink and then she put on her coat again.

'I'm going to the hospital,' she said.

Then she took hold of Kingshaw and held his face against her coat. 'Oh Charles,' she said. 'Why did you do it? Why did you climb the castle?'

She stood looking round the room for a moment and then ran out to the car.

When the car had gone, Kingshaw began to tremble.

'Hooper is dead,' he said, 'Hooper is dead.'

Darkness came and Kingshaw went to bed. But he could not

sleep. He was alone in the house. He was the King of the Castle. He did not have to go to Hooper's school now. Everything was all right. He would have his mother and Mr Hooper. He was the King of the Castle, the King the King ...

At last he went to sleep. Then he had dreams ...

When Kingshaw woke up, he was sweating and crying. He ran down the stairs crying out for his mother.

Mr Hooper came into the hall. He picked Kingshaw up and carried him to a chair. Kingshaw went on crying.

'Hooper's dead,' he said. 'He fell and he's dead ...'

But Mr Hooper and Mrs Kingshaw laughed. 'No, no,' Mrs Kingshaw said. 'Edmund's not dead!'

Kingshaw was carried back to bed. Hooper was not dead. Hooper was not dead. He had not killed him! Kingshaw fell asleep.

But when he woke up, he was afraid again.

'Hooper is not dead,' he said aloud. 'Hooper is not dead. What will he do to me now?'

It was a long time before he went to sleep again.

15

Fielding

Hooper was in hospital. He had been in hospital for a week. Kingshaw went into Hooper's room and took a jigsaw[44]. He began to play with it. His mother came into the room, wearing her coat.

'I am going to see Edmund,' she said. 'Will you come with me?'

'No,' said Kingshaw.

'Why not?'

'I don't want to.'

Mrs Kingshaw looked angry. Then she smiled. 'Why don't you want to see Edmund? He's your friend,' she said.

'Hooper is not my friend.'

'But he soon will be.'

'I hate him,' Kingshaw replied. 'I wish he was dead.'

Mrs Kingshaw went away and he was left alone. Kingshaw looked at a model he had made. He had made a model castle. He was very pleased with it.

Kingshaw took the jigsaw back into Hooper's room.

'I shouldn't have taken it,' he said. 'I shouldn't have gone into his room. Hooper will know. He always knows.'

Kingshaw left the house and went for a walk. Soon he came to an old church and he went inside.

'Oh God,' he said. 'I'm sorry. I wanted Hooper to die. Please make everything all right.'

Kingshaw got up and turned round. A boy was standing there. He was a thin boy, about eleven years old.

'My name's Fielding,' said the boy. 'You live with the Hoopers, don't you? I know all about you. I've seen your mother. We see everything from our farm.'

The boys went outside.

'Would you like to see our farm?' Fielding asked.

Kingshaw followed Fielding to the farm. Fielding stopped outside a shed.

'Would you like to see our new calf[45]?' he asked.

Kingshaw and Fielding went inside. The calf was very young. It was a few hours old. It was lying with its mother.

Fielding showed him the other animals on the farm. Then they walked back through the fields. Kingshaw told Fielding about Hooper. Fielding laughed.

'He can't hurt you. You shouldn't be scared of him,' he said. 'I have to go back to the farm now,' he said. 'Come and see me soon.'

'Thanks,' said Kingshaw. 'I will.'

Kingshaw went home, running and jumping. He felt stronger and more happy. He had found a friend!

When he arrived at the door of the house, his mother was there.

'Oh, Charles,' she said. 'Everything's going to be all right. Edmund is coming home tomorrow.'

16

Hooper Comes Home

When Hooper arrived home, Kingshaw was made to go and talk to him.

Hooper looked at Kingshaw. 'You've been into my room,' he said.

Kingshaw was frightened. How did Hooper know?

'You took my jigsaw,' said Hooper. 'You took it without asking me. That's stealing.'

Kingshaw did not reply. He looked at Hooper. Hooper had broken his leg and two of his ribs. He was in bed. He could not walk.

I wish Hooper was dead, Kingshaw thought. Then he felt ashamed.

'Does your leg hurt?' he asked Hooper.

For a moment, Hooper was quiet. Then he said, 'Something will happen to you, Kingshaw. Something bad.'

'You don't frighten me, Hooper!'

Hooper smiled and looked at Kingshaw. Kingshaw knew that Hooper was right. He knew what was going to happen. Hooper would wait until they were at school. Then it would all begin.

'I know about a boy called Fielding,' said Hooper quietly. 'I know everything. Your mother tells me lots of things about you.'

Kingshaw wanted to cry. Hooper knew. Hooper had found out everything. Then Hooper picked up something from the side of the bed.

It was Kingshaw's model of the castle.

Kingshaw looked at the castle for a moment. Then he ran downstairs, trembling with anger.

'It's my model!' he shouted to his mother and Mr Hooper.

'You gave him my model. You didn't ask me! Make him give

59

it back to me,' Kingshaw shouted again. 'He's got lots of things. He's got everything.'

'Charles ...' said his mother.

'It's mine, mine, mine! He mustn't have anything of mine!'

Mr Hooper stepped forward and hit Kingshaw on the face. None of them moved and no one spoke.

Then the telephone rang. Mr Hooper left the room.

'Go upstairs,' said his mother. 'You've made me very unhappy.' Kingshaw did not look at her.

Kingshaw went to Hooper's room and pushed the door open with his foot. He was breathing quickly.

'Give it to me,' he said to Hooper.

Hooper looked up.

'It's mine!' shouted Kingshaw.

'Your mother gave it to me,' said Hooper.

'I don't care. It's mine.'

'You made it in our house,' Hooper said. 'You made it with our things. So it isn't yours, it's mine. Nothing in this house is yours.'

Kingshaw began to walk towards the bed. 'Give it to me,' he said.

Hooper held the model above his head.

'I'll hit you, Hooper!'

'You daren't touch me, Kingshaw. I'm ill.'

Kingshaw tried to take the castle. Hooper threw it across the room. It hit the wall and fell to the floor. Kingshaw got down and picked up the broken model. Mrs Kingshaw came into the room.

'Charles,' she said. 'I think you should be very, very ashamed of yourself.'

17

Bad News

Mr Hooper was a lonely man. His first marriage had not been happy. He had not loved his wife.

But Mrs Kingshaw was different. She was interested in what he said. And she would make him happy.

'I will tell her tomorrow,' he said to himself. 'I will ask her to marry me.'

Kingshaw was making a new model when Hooper came into the room.

'Don't touch my model,' said Kingshaw.

'I don't like your model. It's stupid,' said Hooper. Then he said, 'I've got a secret. You won't like it.'

Kingshaw waited.

'My father is going to marry your mother,' said Hooper. 'They're going to marry before we go back to school. I heard them talking about it. I knew it was going to happen.'

Kingshaw did not speak for a moment. Then he said, 'Go away, Hooper. I don't want to talk to you.'

'You will have to do what my father says, Kingshaw.'

'Shut up.'

'And you'll have to do what I say too,' said Hooper. And he left the room.

That night, Kingshaw sat in his bed crying. There was nothing he could do. He would have to go to Hooper's school. He would have to live in this ugly old house with Mr Hooper. He would have to live in these dark rooms for ever. Then he began to think about

Fielding. Fielding was his friend. If Fielding was there everything would be all right. At last Kingshaw fell asleep.

———

The next day, Kingshaw's mother came to his room. She was smiling happily.

'I've been to see Mrs Fielding,' she said.

Kingshaw looked at his mother. He was afraid of what she was going to say.

'I met Mrs Fielding last week. I've been to the farm today.'

'Why? You shouldn't have gone there.'

'Don't speak to me like that, Charles. I asked Anthony Fielding to come and have tea with us.'

'I don't want him to come here.'

'Charles, I thought you liked him.'

Kingshaw was very angry with his mother. She did not understand anything.

'He's my friend,' Kingshaw said, 'and he won't want to come here.'

'But he told me he wanted to come here,' said Mrs Kingshaw.

Kingshaw went out of the house. He thought about Fielding and the farm. Now Hooper knew about them. Hooper would take Fielding away from him. Hooper had everything now.

———

That afternoon, Fielding came to tea. Afterwards the three boys walked across the hall.

Hooper spoke to Fielding. 'I want to show you something in the Red Room.'

'What?'

'You might not like it. You might be scared.'

Fielding was surprised. 'I don't get frightened,' he said.

'Kingshaw's scared,' said Hooper.

Fielding stopped. 'We won't go in then.'

'You can do what you like,' said Kingshaw. 'I don't care.'

'Is it something alive?' asked Fielding.

'No,' said Hooper. 'They're dead things.'

'There's nothing to be afraid of then,' said Fielding. Then he looked at Kingshaw. 'But if ...'

'I don't care what you do,' said Kingshaw. He was angry.

Inside the Red Room, Fielding gave a shout. 'Butterflies! Great!'

'Moths,' said Hooper. 'Moths are different.'

Fielding looked down at the glass cases.

'My grandfather collected them,' said Hooper. 'They're very valuable. My father could sell them for thousands of pounds.'

'That's a lie!' said Kingshaw.

Hooper turned to Kingshaw. 'You're scared of them,' he said. 'You don't know anything.'

Hooper looked at Fielding. 'I dare you to touch one of the animals!' he said.

'Why not?' Fielding said. 'They're dead. They can't hurt me.'

Fielding touched one of the stuffed animals. Then he looked at his hand. It was dirty. 'These things need cleaning,' he said.

'Do you like them?' Hooper asked.

'They smell,' Fielding said.

'Let's go upstairs,' Hooper said. 'I'll show you my map of a battle. And I've got another thing, too.'

The crow, thought Kingshaw, the stuffed crow. They might lock me in the room.

'Kingshaw's afraid,' Hooper said.

'Shut up, Hooper,' said Kingshaw. 'I'll hit you!'

Fielding looked at both of the boys in surprise. Hooper turned away from Kingshaw. 'Come on,' he said to Fielding.

Kingshaw stood and watched them.

'Are you coming?' said Fielding quietly.

Kingshaw said nothing.

'We won't go then,' said Fielding.

'He's scared.' Hooper said. 'Come on, Fielding. I want to show you something interesting.'

Fielding stood for a moment. Then he ran down the stairs.

'I've got a great idea,' he said. 'We'll all go to the farm.'

He ran out into the sunlight and Hooper followed him. Kingshaw stood outside the door and looked down at the ground. He was not going to the farm. If Hooper was going there, Kingshaw did not want to see the farm again.

Fielding waited for Kingshaw but Kingshaw did not move. Then Kingshaw went back into the house and shut the door.

'Come on,' said Hooper. 'Don't wait for Kingshaw. He's stupid. Let's go to your farm.'

They began to walk through the long, wet grass.

Kingshaw went up to Hooper's bedroom. He took Hooper's map of the battle and went outside into the garden. Slowly and carefully, he tore up the map. It took a long time. Then he burnt it.

Kingshaw stood for a moment in the garden. In five days, he would be going to Hooper's school. He was afraid.

It began to rain.

18

The End

Hooper came back from the farm. Later he went up to his room. Kingshaw waited, but nothing happened. Then Hooper came down and looked at him. He did not say anything but Kingshaw was very frightened.

That night, Kingshaw thought about the first day he had come to the house. He remembered his fight with Hooper.

Kingshaw went to sleep. He woke up suddenly in the night. There was a strange sound. He moved in his bed and looked for the stuffed crow. But there was nothing there. Then the sound came again. It was outside his room. Kingshaw waited.

At last, he turned on the light and got out of bed. He saw some paper lying on the floor. He picked it up: SOMETHING WILL HAPPEN TO YOU, KINGSHAW was written on the paper.

Kingshaw dropped the paper. He slowly got back into bed. Kingshaw covered his face, then he began to tremble.

———

Kingshaw woke up very early. He knew what he was going to do. He walked downstairs and went outside.

It was cold and wet outside, but the rain had stopped. He climbed over a fence and began to walk across a field.

He walked into Hang Wood. The wood was cold and dark but Kingshaw was happy. He was safe there.

After a long time, Kingshaw found the clearing. The stones were there, where they had left them.

He took his clothes off and put them carefully on the bank of the stream. The water was very cold and he shivered. He began to think about Hooper and the new school. He thought about his mother and Mr Hooper. He walked into the middle of the stream. Then he lay down slowly and put his face under the water. He breathed very slowly and carefully ...

———

Hooper found him. Hooper knew where to look. They all followed Hooper and shouted loudly. It was raining and the trees and bushes were wet.

Hooper saw Kingshaw's body in the water.

I've won, thought Hooper. Kingshaw is dead.

Mrs Kingshaw took hold of Hooper and held him.

'I don't want you to look, Edmund,' she said. 'Everything will be all right.'

Hooper felt her coat against his face. He smiled. Then there was the sound of the men, moving through the water towards Kingshaw's body.

POINTS
FOR
UNDERSTANDING

Points for Understanding

1

1 'Your grandfather is very old and he is dying,' Mr Hooper said to
Edmund.
    (a) Where will Edmund live when his grandfather dies?
    (b) Who will own his grandfather's house one day?
2 Edmund opened the door to the Red Room. What did he see?
3 Edmund touched the large moth in the middle of the case.
    (a) What happened to the moth?
    (b) What did Edmund think of?
4 'I don't want a friend,' Edmund told his father.
    (a) Who was coming to live with the Hoopers?
    (b) How old was the friend?
5 Mr Hooper looked at Edmund and remembered his wife.
    (a) When did Mrs Hooper die?
    (b) Was the marriage a happy one?

2

1 What was Edmund doing when the Kingshaws arrived?
2 Edmund threw a note out of the window to Charles Kingshaw.
    (a) What was fixed to the paper to make it fall on the ground?
    (b) What did Edmund say in the note?
3 Edmund told Charles Kingshaw a lie about his grandfather.
    (a) What did he say?
    (b) Why did he tell the lie?

3

1 Kingshaw was very unhappy in the house. Hooper was unkind to him and
followed him everywhere. One day Kingshaw found a map. Where did he
decide to go first?
2 While he was running, Kingshaw fell to the ground. He was very frightened.
Why was he frightened?
3 Kingshaw climbed over a fence and ran to the house. Who did he see when
he looked up at the house?

4

1 Hooper knew that Kingshaw was afraid of many things. What did Hooper dare Kingshaw to do?
2 Kingshaw woke up in the night.
    (a) What was on his bed?
    (b) Who put it there?

5

1 After supper, Hooper took Kingshaw to the Red Room. Hooper asked Kingshaw to open one of the cases.
    (a) Why did Kingshaw refuse to open the case?
    (b) What did Hooper do suddenly?
2 What happened when Kingshaw switched on the light in the Red Room?
3 That night, Kingshaw lay in bed thinking. He wanted three things to happen. What were they?

6

1 Kingshaw found a secret room in the house. But he knew that Hooper would find the secret room. So he made a plan. What was the plan?
2 Hooper guessed Kingshaw's plan. What did Hooper say he would do?
3 Mr Hooper and Mrs Kingshaw spent more and more time together.
    (a) Why did Mr Hooper like Mrs Kingshaw?
    (b) Why was Mrs Kingshaw pleased she had come to live in the house?
4 Why was Kingshaw ashamed of his mother?

7

1 Kingshaw decided to run away.
    (a) What did he put in his bag?
    (b) How much money did he have?
2 Why did he decide to walk across the fields?
3 Why did Kingshaw have to go to Hang Wood?
4 Who followed Kingshaw into Hang Wood? What did Kingshaw want to do?

5 'We're lost,' said Kingshaw.
   (a) What did Hooper start to do?
   (b) What sound did they hear in the distance?

8

1 Hooper's face was very white. 'Thunderstorms make me ill,' he said.
  What did Kingshaw learn about Hooper?
2 'I can hear a stream,' said Kingshaw. 'I want a drink. I'm going to find
  the stream.'
   (a) What did Hooper do then?
   (b) Why was Kingshaw surprised?
3 What did the boys find in the clearing?

9

1 'We must make a fire,' said Kingshaw. Why did they want to have a
  fire?
2 How did Hooper try to make Kingshaw afraid?

10

1 Why did Hooper start screaming?
2 What did Kingshaw do to make Hooper stop screaming?
3 Why did Kingshaw tie the string to a tree?
4 What did Kingshaw find when he got back to the clearing?
5 What happened to Hooper? How did Kingshaw make him breathe
  again?
6 What did they eat for supper?
7 'That's a lie!' shouted Kingshaw.
   (a) What had Hooper said?
   (b) Did Kingshaw really believe it was a lie?

11

1 What did the boys eat for breakfast?
2 Kingshaw remembered what Hooper had said and done. Why did
  Kingshaw think everything might be all right?

3 When they got back to the house Hooper told his father lies. What did he say?
4 Did Mrs Kingshaw believe what Charles said?
5 'Mr Hooper and I have a surprise for you, Charles,' said Mrs Kingshaw. What did Kingshaw think the surprise was?

12

1 The next day, Mr Hooper told Kingshaw what the surprise was. What was going to happen?
2 What did Kingshaw do when he heard the news?
3 Hooper locked Kingshaw in an old shed. Kingshaw fell asleep. What did he dream about?
4 'You're coming to my school,' said Hooper. 'I have many friends there.'
    (a) What did Hooper say his friends would do to Kingshaw?
    (b) What did Kingshaw say he would tell Hooper's friends?

13

1 They reached Leydell Castle.
    (a) Where did Mr Hooper take Mrs Kingshaw?
    (b) Where did the boys run to?
    (c) What did Kingshaw say he was going to do?
2 What did Kingshaw shout out when he got to the top of the wall?
3 Hooper tried to climb up the castle wall.
    (a) What happened when Kingshaw asked him to climb down again?
    (b) What happened when Kingshaw tried to help him to climb down?

14

1 Hooper was lifted into the ambulance. What did Kingshaw think had happened to Hooper?
2 Why did Kingshaw think that everything was all right?
3 Why was Kingshaw afraid when he learned that Hooper was not dead?

15

1 Mrs Kingshaw asked Charles to go with her to the hospital. What did Kingshaw say?
2 'Would you like to see our farm?' Fielding said.
    (a) Who was Fielding?
    (b) How old was he?
    (c) What did Fielding take Kingshaw to see?
3 Why was Kingshaw happy?

16

1 What was the first thing Hooper said to Kingshaw when he came home?
2 Who had told Hooper about Fielding?
3 Why did Hooper say the model castle was his? What did Hooper do to the model castle?

17

1 'I've got a secret,' Hooper told Kingshaw. 'You won't like it.'
    (a) What was the secret?
    (b) Why did Kingshaw sit in his bed crying?
2 Why did Kingshaw not want Fielding to come to the house?
3 Why did Hooper take Fielding into the Red Room and show him the moths?
4 Hooper dared Fielding to touch one of the stuffed animals. What was Fielding's reply?
5 Why did Kingshaw not go to the farm with Hooper and Fielding.
6 What did Kingshaw do in Hooper's bedroom?
7 What was going to happen in five days? Why was Kingshaw afraid?

18

1 That night, a piece of paper was pushed under Kingshaw's bedroom door. What was written on the paper?
2 Where did Kingshaw go to in Hang Wood?
3 'I don't want you to look, Edmund,' said Mrs Kingshaw.
    (a) What did she not want Hooper to look at?
    (b) Why did Hooper say to himself: 'I've won.'?

GLOSSARY

Glossary

1 **wood** (page 6)
   a large number of trees growing together.
2 **ceiling** (page 6)
   you walk on the floor in a room. The ceiling is above your head.
3 **hall** (page 6)
   the hall is inside the front door of a house. Doors open from the hall into other rooms.
4 **museum** (page 6)
   a building where old and beautiful things are kept. People visit museums to see the things which are kept there.
5 **glass case** (page 6)
   a large wooden box with a glass top so that you can see inside.
6 **moths and butterflies** (page 6)
   insects which fly. Some moths and butterflies have very beautiful wings.
7 **stuffed animals** (page 6)
   the skins of dead animals and birds that have been kept in a special way. The skins are taken off the bodies of the animals and birds and filled with special material. Stuffed animals and birds look as if they are alive.
8 **famous collector** (page 6)
   Edmund's grandfather kept dead butterflies and moths in glass cases. He had a very large collection of insects. People came to see this collection. He became a famous collector.
9 **argue** (page 7)
   to disagree with someone about something.
10 **make a map** (page 8)
   to draw on paper the positions of rivers, mountains, roads, towns, etc. Edmund was making a map of a battle. His map showed the two armies of soldiers who were fighting each other.
11 **plasticine** (page 8)
   a soft sticky material that children play with. It can easily be made into different shapes.
12 **scared** (page 10)
   to be frightened or afraid of something or someone.
13 **valuable** (page 10)
   worth a lot of money.

14 **lie** (page 10)
    to tell a lie is to say something which is untrue.
15 **boarding school** (page 11)
    see the Note About This Story on page 4.
16 **ashamed** (page 11)
    to feel unhappy because you or someone else has done something
    wrong or foolish.
17 **wipe** (page 11)
    Kingshaw rubbed his hands across his face to take away the blood.
18 **corn** (page 13)
    plants grown for food. Bread is made from the seed of the corn.
19 **sweat** (page 13)
    when you are very hot or afraid, water comes out of your skin. This
    water is called sweat.
20 **crow** (page 13)
    a large black bird.
21 **dive** (page 13)
    the bird stopped flying round and suddenly came down towards
    Kingshaw.
22 **scream** (page 14)
    to shout out loudly when you are very frightened.
23 **fence** (page 14)
    a line of wooden posts and wire round a field. Fences keep animals
    in the fields. They also show which piece of land a person owns.
24 **tremble** (page 14)
    when you are ill or afraid, your body trembles or shakes.
25 **dare someone to do something** (page 16)
    to tell someone to do something which is frightening or dangerous.
    Hooper knows that Kingshaw is afraid of the wood. He dares him
    to go into the wood. He does not think Kingshaw will go. Children
    often dare each other to do something dangerous or frightening.
26 **model** (page 23)
    Kingshaw has made a ship. The ship looks exactly like a real ship,
    but it is very much smaller.
27 **feel safe** (page 23)
    to feel happy and comfortable.
28 **secret** (page 23)
    Kingshaw had found a room where no one went. He told no one
    about the room. He kept the room secret from everyone else.

29 **run away** (page 23)
to leave home without telling anyone.
30 **stole** (page 24)
to steal is to take something which does not belong to you.
31 **shiver** (page 27)
when you are very cold or afraid your body shakes. You shiver. See tremble. Gloss. No. 24.
32 **ditch** (page 27)
a long, deep hole which goes along beside a field.
33 **clearing** (page 29)
an open space in the wood where there are no trees or bushes.
34 **thunder** (page 30)
the loud noise you hear during a storm before the rain falls.
35 **stream** (page 32)
a small river.
36 **muddy** (page 33)
when the ground is soft and wet, it is muddy.
37 **bank** (page 34)
where the ground goes down to the water of a stream.
38 **make a mistake** (page 34)
to do something wrong. Kingshaw knew that Hooper did not like being told what to do. Hooper would become angry. -
39 **aspirin** (page 40)
a medicine you take to stop pain or a fever.
40 **shed** (page 46)
a small building made of wood or metal.
41 **ruins** (page 49)
the broken walls and rooms of an old building. There are many ruined castles in England. Many people go to see them every year.
42 **lake** (page 49)
a very large pool of water.
43 **King of the Castle** (page 50)
see the Note About This Story on page 4.
44 **jigsaw** (page 56)
a children's toy. A jigsaw is made of different shaped pieces of wood or cardboard. You put the pieces together to make a picture.
45 **calf** (page 57)
a young cow or bull.

Shane *by Jack Schaefer*
Old Mali and the Boy *by D. R. Sherman*
Bristol Murder *by Philip Prowse*
Tales of Goha *by Leslie Caplan*
The Smuggler *by Piers Plowright*
The Pearl *by John Steinbeck*
Things Fall Apart *by Chinua Achebe*
The Woman Who Disappeared *by Philip Prowse*
The Moon is Down *by John Steinbeck*
A Town Like Alice *by Nevil Shute*
The Queen of Death *by John Milne*
Walkabout *by James Vance Marshall*
Meet Me in Istanbul *by Richard Chisholm*
The Great Gatsby *by F. Scott Fitzgerald*
The Space Invaders *by Geoffrey Matthews*
My Cousin Rachel *by Daphne du Maurier*
I'm the King of the Castle *by Susan Hill*
Dracula *by Bram Stoker*
The Sign of Four *by Sir Arthur Conan Doyle*
The Speckled Band and Other Stories *by Sir Arthur Conan Doyle*
The Eye of the Tiger *by Wilbur Smith*
The Queen of Spades and Other Stories *by Aleksandr Pushkin*
The Diamond Hunters *by Wilbur Smith*
When Rain Clouds Gather *by Bessie Head*
Banker *by Dick Francis*
No Longer at Ease *by Chinua Achebe*
The Franchise Affair *by Josephine Tey*
The Case of the Lonely Lady *by John Milne*

For further information on the full selection of
Readers at all five levels in the series, please refer
to the Macmillan Readers catalogue.

Published by Macmillan Heinemann ELT
Between Towns Road, Oxford OX4 3PP
Macmillan Heinemann ELT is an imprint of
Macmillan Publishers Limited
Companies and representatives troughout the world

ISBN 0 435 27222 5

This retold version by Jim Alderson for Macmillan Guided Readers
First published 1982
Text © Jim Alderson 1982, 1992, 1998, 2002
Design and illustration © Macmillan Publishers Limited 1998, 2002
Heinemann is a registered trademark of Reed Educational & Professional Publishing Limited
This version first published 2002

Illustrated by Bob Harvey
Cover by Richard Parent and Threefold Design

Printed in China

2006 2005 2004 2003 2002
15 14 13 12 11 10 9 8 7 6